Reading About
THE PEREGRINE FALCON

Carol Greene

Content Consultant:
Dan Wharton, Ph.D., Curator,
New York Zoological Society

Reading Consultant:
Michael P. French, Ph.D.,
Bowling Green State University

ENSLOW PUBLISHERS, INC.
Bloy St. & Ramsey Ave.
Box 777
Hillside, N.J. 07205
U.S.A.

P.O. Box 38
Aldershot
Hants GU12 6BP
U.K.

Library of Congress Cataloging-in-Publication Data
Greene, Carol.
    Reading about the peregrine falcon   / Carol Greene.
       p. cm. — (Friends in danger series)
    Includes index.
    Summary: Describes the peregrine falcon and its behavior, explains
its status as an endangered species, and suggests what can be done
to help save it.
    ISBN 0-89490-422-1
    1. Peregrine falcon—Juvenile literature. 2. Rare birds—Juvenile
literature. [1. Peregrine falcon. 2. Falcons. 3. Rare birds.]
I. Title. II. Series: Greene, Carol. Friends in danger series.
QL696.F34G75 1993
598'.918—dc20   92-26804
                                                                 CIP
                                                                  AC

Printed in the United States of America

10 9 8 7 6 5 4 3 2 1

Photo Credits: ©Steve Allen/Gamma Liaison Network, p. 6; © Gerry Ellis/The Wildlife
Collection, pp. 8, 16, 24; © Jacana/Photo Researchers, Inc., p. 12; ©Frans Lanting/Photo
Researchers, Inc., p. 20; ©Brian Parker/Tom Stack & Associates, p. 1; ©LW Richard-
son/Photo Researchers, Inc., p. 22; ©Wendy Shattil/Bob Kozinski/Tom Stack &
Associates, pp. 4, 14; ©Bruce Stoddard, pp. 10, 26; ©Norm Thomas/Photo Researchers,
Inc., p. 18.

Cover Photo Credit: ©Martin Harvey/The Wildlife Collection

Photo Researcher: Grace How

CONTENTS

ROCKY AND ZIP

Winter is almost over.

Rocky flies to the place
where he and his mate
had their nest last year.

Rocky's place is on a ledge
of a tall cliff
in the wild.

A peregrine falcon perches high on a cliff.

Zip flies to the place
where he and his mate
had their nest last year.

Zip's place is on a ledge
of a tall building
in the city.

Rocky and Zip
are peregrine falcons.
They are about 15 inches long.
They weigh about a pound.

A peregrine falcon soars over Park Avenue
in New York City.

In three weeks,
their mates will come.
They are about 20 inches long.
They weigh about two pounds.

Each falcon scrapes out
a clear place
in the sand or rocks.
That is their nest.
Then the female lays eggs.
In April or May,
the chicks will hatch.

A peregrine falcon keep its eggs warm.

Rocky and Zip help
their mates care
for the chicks.
Sometimes they sit
on the nest.
Sometimes they hunt for food.

Rocky and Zip
fly high and fast—
from 40 to 60 miles an hour.

When they see a bird flying
beneath them, they dive.
In a dive, they can go
up to 200 miles an hour.
That makes them
the fastest birds in the world.

Peregrine falcons almost always hunt from
the air.

Rocky hunts doves, ducks,
and other birds in the wild.
Zip hunts pigeons, sparrows,
and other birds in the city.
Their mates hunt too.

They catch the bird with
their sharp claws, or talons.
They use their curved beak
to break the bird's neck.
The bird dies at once.

Then Rocky and Zip
use their strong feet
to carry the bird back
to their hungry chicks.

A peregrine falcon rests on a bird it has
just killed.

When the chicks are
five or six weeks old,
they learn to fly.
They follow their parents
and learn to hunt.

By fall, they will be
on their own.

Peregrine chicks grow fast.

DANGER!

Once, peregrine falcons
lived all over the world.
Three kinds lived in the wild
in North America.

Then, in the 1960s,
they began to disappear.
Here is why.

At one time there were thousands of
peregrine falcons in North America.

People sprayed a poison
called DDT on their farms
to kill insect pests.
Birds ate the dead insects.
The DDT didn't kill the birds.
But it stayed in their bodies.

Peregrine falcons
ate the birds.
Now the DDT was
in their bodies.
It made the females
lay eggs with weak shells.

A plane spreading insect poison across
a farm.

When the falcons
sat on the eggs,
the shells broke.
The chicks could not hatch.

So scientists took the eggs
as soon as they were laid.
They hatched them
in warm machines
called incubators.

Sometimes they put the chicks
back into their nests.
Sometimes they raised
the chicks, then let them go.

Scientists feed peregrine falcon chicks
with hand puppets.

The scientists let some
falcons go in cities.
The falcons liked
their new homes.
They came back each year.

People in North America
don't use DDT anymore.
That helps the falcons.

A scientist gets ready to let go a
peregrine falcon.

But people in Central and
South America do use DDT.
Some of the birds falcons eat
spend the winters there.
They bring the DDT
back in their bodies.

So peregrine falcons
aren't safe yet.
They won't be until
people everywhere
work together
to clean up the earth.

Peregrine falcons are slowly returning to the
cliffs of the western United States.

WHAT YOU CAN DO

1. Learn more about
   peregrine falcons.
   Read books and watch
   nature shows.

2. Learn more about how
   poisons hurt the earth.

3. Talk with your family
   about any poisons
   around your house.
   Look for better ways
   to kill insect pests.

A newborn chick cries for food.

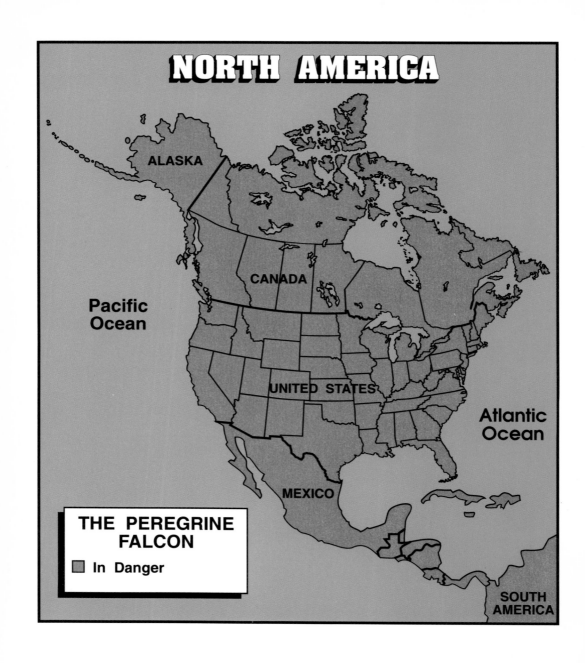

NORTH AMERICA

ALASKA

CANADA

Pacific
Ocean

UNITED STATES

Atlantic
Ocean

MEXICO

THE PEREGRINE
FALCON

In Danger

SOUTH
AMERICA

MORE FACTS ABOUT THE PEREGRINE FALCON

◆ Peregrine falcons are related to gyrfalcons, prairie falcons, merlins, and kestrels.

◆ Their pointed wings help them fly fast.

◆ Peregrine falcons have great eyesight too. If your eyesight were as good as theirs, you could read a newspaper from a mile away.

- Male and female peregrine falcons often stay mates for life.

- The female usually lays three eggs each year. The falcon's nest is sometimes called an eyrie. (Eyrie rhymes with hairy.)

- Scientists use peregrine falcon puppets to feed the chicks they raise. They don't want the chicks to get used to people.

WORDS TO LEARN

chick—A baby bird.

cliff—A steep rocky place.

DDT—A poison used to kill insect pests. It is dangerous to other creatures too.

eyrie—The name for a falcon's nest in a high place.

incubator—A machine used to keep eggs warm until they hatch.

ledge—A narrow shelf.

peregrine falcon—A small, fast bird that hunts other birds. Its Latin name is *Falco peregrinus*.

talon—A claw.

INDEX